BINKY

THE SPACE CAT

KIDS CAN PRESS

For all the cats I've loved

Text and illustrations © 2009 Ashley Spires

This edition is only available for distribution through
the school market by Scholastic Canada, Ltd.

ISBN 978-1-55453-585-9

CM PA 09 0 9 8 7 6 5 4 3 2 1

Kids Can Press acknowledges the financial support of the Government of Ontario, through the Ontario
Media Development Corporation's Ontario Book Initiative; the Ontario Arts Council; the Canada
Council for the Arts; and the Government of Canada, through the BPIDP, for our publishing activity.

Published in Canada by
Kids Can Press Ltd.
29 Birch Avenue
Toronto, ON M4V 1E2

Published in the U.S. by
Kids Can Press Ltd.
2250 Military Road
Tonawanda, NY 14150

www.kidscanpress.com

The artwork in this book was rendered
in ink, watercolor and cat fur.
The text is set in Fontoon.

Edited by Tara Walker
Designed by Karen Powers
Printed and bound in China

Kids Can Press is a *corus*™ Entertainment company

The hardcover edition of this book is smyth
sewn casebound.
The paperback edition of this book is limp sewn
with a drawn-on cover.

CM 09 0 9 8 7 6 5 4 3 2 1
CM PA 09 0 9 8 7 6 5 4 3 2

**Library and Archives Canada Cataloguing in
Publication**

Spires, Ashley, 1978–
    Binky the space cat / written and illustrated
by Ashley Spires.

Interest age level: Ages 7 to 10.

ISBN 978-1-55453-309-1 (bound)
ISBN 978-1-55453-419-7 (pbk.)

1. Cats—Juvenile fiction. I. Title.

PS8637.P57B55 2009   jC813'.6   C2009-900736-3

Please note: No aliens, bugs or Space Cats were
harmed in the making of this book. Okay, a mosquito
was batted away a little too enthusiastically, and a
fruit fly drowned under slightly suspicious
circumstances, but that's all.
Space Cat's honor.

BINKY
THE SPACE CAT

by ASHLEY SPIRES

FTTTTTTPT

PLOP

IT FINALLY CAME IN THE MAIL.

Yoink!

HE HAD BEEN WAITING FOR WEEKS.

squeak

click

SOMETHING THIS IMPORTANT REQUIRED COMPLETE PRIVACY.

TINK!

Riiiiiiiiip!

slide

F.U.R.S.T.
Felines of the Universe
Ready for Space Travel

Dear Binky,

We are pleased to announce that you are now Space Cat qualified. Enclosed is all the information you need to pursue an exciting life in space travel.

The following documents are for Space Cat eyes only and deal with super top-secret classified information. F.U.R.S.T. regulations clearly state that anyone caught unlawfully reading super top-secret information may be subject to hissing and scratching.

Sincerely,

Sergeant Fluffy Vandermere

BINKY IS A SPACE CAT.

Space Cat Certified

NAME: Binky
COLOR: Black/White
FUR: Shorthair
BIRTH DATE: 12/07/06

89J43-PW

F.U.R.S.T. Felines of the Universe
Ready for Space Travel

OFFICIAL
SPACE CAT
BADGE

UNLIKE YOUR AVERAGE CAT ...

HE HAS A PURPOSE.

WHOOOSH!

HIS MISSION IS TO ONE DAY BLAST OFF INTO OUTER SPACE ...

ACTUALLY, BINKY HASN'T EVER BEEN OUTSIDE.

TWEET

SWOOSH

sigh

HE LIVES HERE, IN THIS SPACE STATION, ENTIRELY SURROUNDED BY OUTER SPACE.

OUTER SPACE

THAT'S WHY, UNTIL NOW, HE HAS HAD TO STAY INSIDE.

OUTER SPACE ISN'T SAFE FOR AN ORDINARY CAT.

IF BINKY WENT OUTSIDE WITHOUT PROPER PREPARATION, HE WOULDN'T BE ABLE TO BREATHE.

(OUTER SPACE TENDS NOT TO HAVE OXYGEN.)

AND HE WOULD FLOAT AWAY.

(OUTER SPACE IS ALMOST ALWAYS GRAVITY FREE.)

BINKY LIVES WITH ONE BIG HUMAN ...

ONE SMALL HUMAN ...

AND HIS MOUSIE, TED.

BINKY LOVES HIS HUMANS.

Prrrrrrrrrrrrrrrrr

HE TAKES EXTREMELY GOOD CARE OF THEM.

HE GREETS THEM AT THE DOOR.

HE HELPS AROUND THE HOUSE.

HE GIVES THEM MASSAGES.

HE SINGS THEM TO SLEEP.

AND, MOST IMPORTANTLY, **HE PROTECTS THEM FROM ALIENS!!**

IN RETURN, BINKY'S HUMANS FEED HIM WELL ...

MAYBE TOO WELL ...

burp

AND GIVE HIM CUDDLES.

prrrrrrrr

HE MAKES A MENTAL NOTE TO SEND THEM A POSTCARD FROM **OUTER SPACE.**

DESPITE HIS YOUNG AGE, HE QUICKLY REALIZED ...

THAT ALIENS ...

WERE ...

EVERYWHERE!!

bzzzzzzz

19

HE COULD TELL THEY WERE ALIENS
BECAUSE THEY COULD FLY.

Things i know
1. Always use the litter box.
2. Fish smells yummy.
3. Miniskirts are not meant for everyone.
4. Only aliens can fly.
5. Ted is my friend.

EVEN KITTENS KNOW
THAT ONLY ALIENS
CAN FLY.

BINKY ALSO NOTICED THAT HIS HUMANS KEPT REFERRING TO THE ALIENS AS "BUGS."

LIKE ANY CURIOUS KITTEN ...

BINKY DECIDED TO DO SOME RESEARCH.

scritch scratch

ALIEN QUALITIES	BUG QUALITIES
- can fly	- can fly
- have big eyes	- have big eyes
- steal your food	- steal your food
- lay eggs	- lay eggs
- technologically advanced species who have mastered space travel	- eat poo

BINKY DREW THREE CONCLUSIONS:

1. OBVIOUSLY, BUGS AND ALIENS ARE THE SAME THING.

2. TOO BAD HUMANS AREN'T SMART ENOUGH TO FIGURE THIS OUT.

very small

even smaller

3. THAT MUST BE WHY THEY NEED A CAT AROUND.

BINKY HAD NO IDEA WHAT TO DO ABOUT THE ALIEN PROBLEM.

HE WAS JUST A KITTEN AFTER ALL.

HE TRIED A FEW THINGS, BUT NOTHING WORKED.

THEN ONE DAY, HE FOUND SOMETHING AT THE BOTTOM OF HIS KITTY FOOD BAG.

rustle
rustle

munch
munch

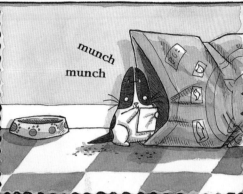

F.U.R.S.T.

Want to stop aliens?
Then become a
SPACE CAT
today!!!

FROM THAT MOMENT ON,
BINKY WAS DETERMINED
TO BE A SPACE CAT.

BINKY'S HUMANS HAVE NO IDEA THAT HE IS NOW A REAL SPACE CAT ...

PROTECTING THEM FROM ALIEN DOMINATION.

(AS MENTIONED EARLIER, THEY AREN'T VERY BRIGHT.)

IT'S IMPERATIVE THAT HIS IDENTITY REMAIN A SECRET.

gasp!

IF ONE OF THE ALIEN SPIES
WERE TO FIND OUT ...

bzzz bzzz
bzzz Space Cat
bzzz bzzz

WHO HE REALLY IS ...

bzzzz
bzzzzzzzzz
bzzzzzzz
bzzzzzz

MEOW!!!

THE ALIENS COULD MOUNT
AN ATTACK ...

bzzzzzzzzzz

THAT EVEN BINKY, AN OFFICIAL
CERTIFIED SPACE CAT, COULDN'T
DEFEAT.

PUNT!

29

AND THEN WHAT?

HE AND HIS HUMANS WOULD BE ENSLAVED BY THE FLYING MENACES AND FORCED TO DO HORRIBLE THINGS ...

GAG!

Ewwww!

BLECH!

LIKE EAT VEGETABLES ...

VRRRRRRRRR

OR STAY IN THE SAME ROOM AS THE VACUUM ...

OR LEAVE THE KITTY LITTER BOX UNSCOOPED!

IT'S ALMOST TOO TERRIBLE TO IMAGINE!

IN ORDER TO PREVENT THIS KIND OF ALIEN INVASION ...

BINKY PATROLS THE PERIMETER.

HE ELIMINATES THE ALIENS WHO ARE DARING ENOUGH ...

TO SNEAK INTO **HIS** SPACE STATION.

GULP!

ONE OF THE BASIC RULES OF BEING A SPACE CAT IS TO CONSTANTLY TRAIN AGAINST ALIEN ATTACKS.

PRETEND ALIEN

KAPOW!

BINKY TRAINS VERY HARD.

HE CAN OUTMANEUVER ...

OUTRUN ...

AND OUTSMART ANY ALIEN CREATURE THAT HE COMES ACROSS.

WELL, ALMOST EVERY ALIEN.

CRASH!

meow

HE DEALS WITH ALIEN INVADERS QUICKLY ...

crunch
crunch

AND THOROUGHLY.

Poooot!

THE REALLY CRUNCHY ONES GIVE HIM SPACE GAS.

ZOOOOOM!

BINKY KNOWS THAT IN ORDER TO SPACE TRAVEL, YOU NEED A ROCKET SHIP ...

SPACE SHIPS!

One small step ...

OR, AT THE VERY LEAST, AN AIRTIGHT ASTRONAUT SUIT.

HE HAS SEEN HIS HUMANS PUT ON THEIR SPECIAL SPACE SUITS WHENEVER THEY GO OUT.

BINKY WORRIES ABOUT HIS HUMANS ...

OUT THERE ALL ALONE ...

AAAAAAAAAAAAA!

MEOW!

WITH NO SPACE CAT TO PROTECT THEM.

ONE DAY HE TRIED ON SOME OF THEIR SPACE GEAR, HOPING HE COULD GO WITH THEM.

trip

MEOW!

bump

CRASH!

IT DIDN'T WORK.

SINCE HE DOESN'T HAVE A SPACE SUIT ...

BINKY HAS NO CHOICE ...

lick
lick

ZIIIP!

BUT TO BUILD HIS OWN **ROCKET SHIP!**

FORTUNATELY, DETAILED ROCKET SHIP BLUEPRINTS ARE INCLUDED WITH EVERY SPACE CAT INTRODUCTORY PACKAGE.

F.U.R.S.T.

You're a Space Cat, Now What?

CHAPTER 3: How to Build a Rocket Ship with Things You Can Steal from Your Humans

SOME PARTS ARE EASIER TO FIND THAN OTHERS ...

BUT BINKY MANAGES TO COLLECT ALL THE NECESSARY COMPONENTS.

PZZZZZZZZZZZZZZZ!

TUCKED AWAY IN HIS LITTER BOX ...

wusha wusha

BINKY PREPARES FOR HIS MISSION.

CLONK!

HIS SHIP IS COMING TOGETHER NICELY.

BZZZZZZ

BUT HE HAS TO BE CAREFUL.

click!

SECRET ROCKET SHIP BLUEPRINTS

crunch

crunch

SWIPE!

YIPES!

THE ENEMY IS ALWAYS WATCHING.

IT'S TIME FOR BINKY TO READY HIMSELF FOR SPACE TRAVEL.

HE USES THE FLIGHT SIMULATOR ...

MEOW!

whirrrr

MEOW!

vrrrrrrrrr

THE G-FORCE REPLICATOR ...

AND THE ZERO-GRAVITY CHAMBER.

MEOW!

ULTRADRY

thumpa
thumpa

DISCLAIMER: BINKY IS A TRAINED SPACE CAT. CATS AND HUMANS SHOULD NEVER GO IN THE DRYER. EVER.

BLAAAACH!

SPACE TRAVEL TRAINING IS NOT EASY.

MEEOOOW!

IT FREQUENTLY LEADS TO HAIR BALLS.

AND SO BINKY TRAINS ...

AND BUILDS ...

AND FIGHTS ...

AND CUDDLES ...

AND TRAINS ...

AND BUILDS ...

AND WASHES ...

AND FIGHTS ...

AND BUILDS ...

AND NAPS ...

AND TRAINS ...

UNTIL FINALLY ONE DAY ...

49

WITH A LITTLE ROCKET FUEL ...

SOME SPACE SNACKS ...

HIS SPACE HELMET ...

AND HIS TRUSTY COPILOT ...

BINKY IS **FINALLY** READY FOR **OUTER SPACE!**

WHEN HE IS ALL STRAPPED IN ...

click

click

BOOP

beep

ping!

COUNTDOWN INITIATED

BINKY THE SPACE CAT STARTS THE COUNTDOWN TO BLASTOFF.

52

HE IS ALL PACKED AND READY TO GO ON THE ADVENTURE OF A LIFETIME.

YET BINKY FEELS LIKE SOMETHING IS MISSING ...

HE'S SURE HE HAS PACKED EVERYTHING.

F.U.R.S.T.

- ☑ space helmet
- ☑ snacks
- ☑ copilot
- ☑ planet guide
- ☑ alien fighting gloves
- ☑ zero-gravity kitty litter

BUT THEN HE REALIZES ...

rustle
rustle

SOMETHING VERY IMPORTANT
IS **NOT** ON HIS LIST.

THE MOST IMPORTANT THING OF ALL ...

HIS HUMANS!!!

bzzzzzzzzzzz

WHAT KIND OF A SPACE CAT WOULD HE BE IF HE LEFT THEM BEHIND?

BINKY KNOWS THERE IS ONLY ONE THING TO DO ...

RUMBLE

RUMBLE

whooosh!

ALL OF BINKY'S DREAMS OF **OUTER SPACE** ADVENTURE HAVE DISAPPEARED OUT THE WINDOW.

VWHOOOSH!

NO MORE EXPLORING NEW WORLDS.

NO MORE ALIEN SPACE CHASES.

NO MORE BINKY, SPACE CAT EXTRAORDINAIRE.

BINKY!

scratch

crunch

Thank goodness you were here, Binky!

CLEARLY, BINKY MADE THE RIGHT CHOICE.

Come here, Brave Kitty!

HIS HUMANS ARE UTTERLY HELPLESS WITHOUT HIM.

PLUS, WHO WOULD GIVE HIM CUDDLES WAY OUT IN **OUTER SPACE?**

PRRRRRRRRRRRRRRRRRRR

BINKY HAS LEARNED SOMETHING VERY IMPORTANT ...

NEXT TIME, BUILD A BIGGER ROCKET SHIP.